W9-APW-358

A TALE FOR

Easter

by

Tasha Tudor

SIMON & SCHUSTER
BOOKS FOR YOUNG READERS
NEW YORK LONDON TORONTO SYDNEY SINGAPORE

SIMON & SCHUSTER

BOOKS FOR YOUNG READERS

An imprint of Simon & Schuster Children's Publishing Division

1230 Avenue of the Americas, New York, New York 10020

Text copyright 1941 by Oxford University Press

Copyright renewed © 1969 by Corgi Cottage, L.L.C.

First Simon & Schuster Books for Young Readers edition, 2001

All rights reserved including the right of reproduction in whole or in part or in any form.

SIMON & SCHUSTER BOOKS FOR YOUNG READERS is a trademark of Simon & Schuster.

Book design by Heather Wood

The text of this book is set in Didot Roman Oldstyle. The illustrations are rendered in watercolor.

Printed in Hong Kong

2 4 6 8 10 9 7 5 3 1

Library of Congress Cataloging-in-Publication Data

Tudor, Tasha.

A tale for Easter / by Tasha Tudor.

p. cm.

Summary : While awaiting the arrival of Easter, a child dreams of rabbits with shining eyes,

little lambs, Easter ducklings, and other wonderful surprises.   ISBN 0-689-82844-6

[1. Easter—Fiction. 2. Animals—Fiction.] I. Title.

PZ7.T8228 Tal 2001   [E]—dc21   99-462167

To

LITTLE ANN NEWELL

You can never tell
what might happen on Easter.

You're not always sure when it is coming,
even though you go to Sunday school.

You can guess it is near

when Mama makes you stand still
while she fits a new dress on you.

But it is only when Good Friday comes,
and you have hot cross buns for tea,

that you know for certain
Easter will be the day after tomorrow.

On Saturday you go
and ask the chickens

to lay you plenty of Easter eggs.

If you have been very good
the whole year through,

the night before Easter
you will dream the loveliest dreams.

One will be about a wee fawn,

who makes you as light as thistledown
and takes you on her back and
gallops through the woods and fields.

She shows you rabbits

smoothing their sleek coats
for Easter morning.

And mice with beady eyes

and shining whiskers.

Little lambs, too,

in fields of buttercups.

And Easter ducklings

swimming among the lily pads.

If you have been especially good
and done nearly everything you have been told,

she will take you up, up,
over the misty moisty clouds,
where the bluebirds dye their feathers,
and the robins find the color for their eggs.

But this is only if you have been good

and can find the stardust on daffodils
with your eyes tight shut.

And when you wake up in the morning

there isn't any fawn at all,
and you are just you again.
But often there are colored eggs in your shoes
or in your best bonnet.

Or a basket of ducklings
beside your bowl of porridge.

There might even be a bunny
in Grandma's rocking chair.

You can never really tell,
for anything might happen
on Easter.